For Audrey and Henry —E.W.

For all birthday cake lovers —I.F.

THIS IS A BORZOI BOOK PUBLISHED BY ALFRED A. KNOPF

Text copyright © 2021 by Edwina Wyatt

Jacket art and interior illustrations copyright © 2021 by Irena Freitas

All rights reserved. Published in the United States by Alfred A. Knopf, an imprint of Random House Children's Books, a division of Penguin Random House LLC, New York.

Knopf, Borzoi Books, and the colophon are registered trademarks of Penguin Random House LLC.

Visit us on the Web! rhcbooks.com

Educators and librarians, for a variety of teaching tools, visit us at RHTeachersLibrarians.com

Library of Congress Cataloging-in-Publication Data
Names: Wyatt, Edwina, author. | Freitas, Irena, illustrator.
Title: It took two wishes / Edwina Wyatt ; illustrated by Irena Freitas.
Description: First edition. | New York : Alfred A. Knopf, 2021. | Summary:
A child counts down to a birthday party that does not go exactly as planned.
Identifiers: LCCN 2019023073 (print) | LCCN 2019023074 (ebook) |
ISBN 978-0-593-11954-9 (hardcover) | ISBN 978-0-593-11955-6 (library binding) |
ISBN 978-0-593-11956-3 (ebook)
Subjects: CYAC: Birthdays—Fiction. | Parties—Fiction. | Counting.
Classification: LCC PZ7.1.W973 It 2021 (print) | LCC PZ7.1.W973 (ebook) | DDC [E]—dc23

The text of this book is set in 16-point Edwardian LT Light.

The illustrations were created using a combination of watercolor and digital techniques.

Book design by Nicole Gastonguay

MANUFACTURED IN CHINA
July 2021
10 9 8 7 6 5 4 3 2 1

First Edition

IT TOOK
TWO WISHES

by Edwina Wyatt

illustrations by Irena Freitas

ALFRED A. KNOPF

New York

It took twelve moons.
Six storms.
Four seasons.
Two inches.
And countless sleeps to happen.

But I waited.

For candles and cake, balloons in the park.
The day when one wish might come true.

It took two hours.
Four minutes.
Seven crayons.
Five smudges.
And half a sandwich
to write the invitations.

But I did.

I drew candles on the cake,
balloons in the park.
And hoped that my wish
would come true.

It took three bowls.
Ten eggs.
One river.
Two mountains.
And eight spoons
to bake the cake.

But I did.

It had strawberry icing and sweet sticky cream.
I would blow out my candles. Squeeze my eyes shut.
And wait for my wish to come true.

It took ten blocks.
Three stops.
One bridge.
Nine stairs.
And six jumps to get to the park.

But we did.

But then . . .

No candles. No cake.
No balloons in the park.
There was nothing
that wishing could do.

But then whimpers and whines.
Two sad, lonely eyes.
Somebody *else* wishing too.

We asked one postman.

Two painters.

Six neighbors.

Three pigeons.

And four ducks.
But nobody knew.

Then . . .

Three knocks on a door.

A hundred footsteps.

A million kisses
and tears at least!

We had strawberry icing and sweet sticky cream.
On that day when two wishes came true.